(oo)-Booo!

# Ghostel

## A short story based on the Board Game

G Clatworthy

*G Clatworthy*

*Marlow Indie Book Fair 2025*

ISBN: 978-1-915516-21-3

# Foreword

I love playing board games so when the opportunity came to write a story based on one, I jumped at it. I hope you enjoy my interpretation of one of my favourite games.

A special thank you to Bevan Clatworthy and Gino Brancazio for allowing me to write a story based on their board game. You are awesome!

If you want to support Gemma, you can find her on www.patreon.com/G_Clatworthy for exclusive first reads of new stories. You can also join her newsletter at www.gemmaclatworthy.com for free stories and follow Gemma on www.instagram.com/gemmaclatworthy, www.facebook.com/gemmaclatworthy or join the reader's group on Facebook: Gemma's book wyrms.

# Chapter 1

## In which an old house is disturbed

The wispy figure drifted through the old house slowly. Sun beams caught stray dust motes that stirred lazily in the breeze from the window. Boo watched the dust dance in slow spirals. It reminded her of parties she used to attend in this very house. She followed a larger piece of dust down the stairs, smiling to herself as she copied its twists and turns.

A voice broke through the sunny afternoon. A voice. Boo stopped suddenly halfway down the staircase. She hadn't heard anyone in the house since…she thought back. Not since some teenagers had broken in a couple of years ago. They hadn't stayed long after dark fell. No one stayed. She shook her head slowly; it was always possible she was hallucinating. She moved forward carefully, eager to hear a human voice after so long.

She entered the faded reception room and jolted to a halt. There were indeed two people standing on the threadbare green carpet. One of them held a glossy brochure with a familiar façade printed in full colour on the front page. He wore a suit with close fitting trousers and a pale pink shirt with the top two buttons undone in the hot weather. Boo moved closer.

"So, you see, this will make a perfect addition to your portfolio…" The speaker was an enthusiastic woman in a printed dress. Her long red nails fluttered as she gestured around the room, taking in the musty fireplace and dusty pictures, "it's full of period features and, if that's not up your alley, then you can always rip it down and replace it with a high rise."

The man turned around, taking in the distressed grandeur. "I heard there was a killing…?"

The woman smiled but the warmth didn't reach her brown eyes. "You've certainly done your research and

2

yes, there was an unsavoury event, but it was decades ago. Gone and forgotten. Nothing that would trouble you."

"Hmm," the man grunted non-committally and paced to the next room. Boo moved aside to avoid brushing his suit. The man paused and turned, staring straight at her. Boo stared back. He couldn't see her, she repeated to herself. But still, his sharp eyes looked directly at where she was standing.

"Something wrong Mr Johnson?" The lady moved closer. The smell of her perfume was overwhelming in the stuffy room.

"Nothing. Let's see the rest of this place, then." The man continued to the pale-yellow drawing room. Boo followed, barely able to contain her excitement. People in the house! And one of them had looked at her! She watched as they moved from room to room, trailing their steps in the thick layer of dust. Eventually they ended back at the large wooden front door.

"So, what do you think? It's everything I promised, isn't it?" the woman enthused. Boo had to admire her positivity. Thin cracks ran across the wall like spider webs, and the persistent sunlight had showed up all the flaws in the old building.

Mr Johnson pulled a pair of designer sunglasses from his pocket and tapped them twice against his open palm. "I'll have to send in a structural engineer before I consider anything."

The lady smiled wolfishly and linked her arm through his. "Of course, let's talk details. I know a lovely wine bar just around the corner…"

The door closed behind them with a loud click. The real estate agent didn't even bother to lock it behind her. Boo moved to the window and watched them walk up the path to the iron gates. She considered following them to the brick wall that marked the edge of the property and the boundary she was forced to live within. Instead, she turned and raced upstairs to the attic where she knew she'd find the others.

"There were people!" She burst out as she entered the attic at the top of the Victorian property.

"Whatchoo talking about now, Boo?" Creak propped himself up on the chaise longue he had been reclining on. He was barely more substantial than the shadows gathered behind him.

"People! Humans! In the house! Can you believe it?"

Giggle floated over and looked into Boo's translucent eyes. "People hey? You sure you're not trying to prank us…you know that's my job."

Boo moved back and nodded, trying not to notice the crazy glint that had entered Giggle's eyes. His nickname sounded quaint, but his ability to let out his manic laugh while doing the dirtiest jobs was plain spooky – pardon the pun. Boo held up her hands as if she could physically distance herself from the creep. "I ain't lying! There was people here!"

"What were they like? What did they say?" The ghosts crowded round her. Boo glowed in the centre of their attention.

"More importantly, what were they doing here?" Spookie's voice boomed from the other side of the attic.

The ghosts melted to the sides of the room, leaving Boo alone in the middle. She swallowed, a reflex from her living days. "Er, the lady was showing a fella around the place. I think she was trying to sell it."

"Sell my house?!"

"Sorry boss." Boo hung her head and looked at the floor. She felt his power crackle through the fabric of the air as he moved closer to her.

"It's not your fault. There's always those who want to interfere in my business. You did good, kid." He put an incorporeal hand beneath her chin and lifted her face. She forced herself to meet his gaze. He was smiling. She returned his grin nervously, held in place by the intensity of his dark eyes. "So, what can you tell me about the schmuck who wants to buy this place?"

"Boss?"

"Well, he must be a schmuck if he's interested in this house." The larger ghost couldn't quite keep the echo of desire from his voice.

Boo laughed uncertainly. The others joined in. "He was tall and had a suit with piercing blue eyes…"

"Sheesh Boo, I don't want his dating profile! What did he want?"

"I don't know, boss, I'm sorry. Maybe they'll come back, and I can find out more."

"Yeah…maybe…" He didn't sound convinced.

"There was one thing…" Boo paused, and the boss motioned for her to continue, "…the man…he looked at me."

There was a pause as the ghosts shuffled uncomfortably in the musty room. Then, as one, they let out a series of groans.

"You know the fleshies can't see you."

Boo crossed her arms. "I know what I saw. He looked straight at me."

"Poor little Boo, so desperate she's imagining a fleshy boyfriend! Hey, if you want someone to hold you tight, I'll happily oblige." Giggle made an obscene gesture accompanied with his eerie laughter. Tinker glared at him.

"Cut it out!" The largest ghost's voice broke through the merriment.

"Sorry boss."

"It's not me you need to say sorry to…"

"Sorry Boo."

Boo stuck her tongue out at Giggle while the boss was looking away. The red ghost glared at her.

"Now, Boo," the larger ghost continued, placing an arm around her shoulders, "you know the humans can't see you in the daytime. They can barely see us at night. He was probably looking at something behind you."

Boo nodded disconsolately. He was right. She was just so bored and lonely. Not for the first time, she wondered what she had done to deserve an eternity stuck here.

"Now, let's all keep an eye out for any more humans. We need to know what their plans are and see how we can turn it to our advantage. Yoos all know that old Spookie can turn anything to his advantage..."

# Chapter 2

*In which the ghosts get a glimpse of freedom*

A slow two weeks passed in the old house.

The ghosts had been in a flurry of excitement for the first couple of days. Creak practiced moving objects, dropping old plates and ornaments off every surface until ceramic shards littered the floor. Tinker had stopped the poltergeist from tipping over the old grandfather clock, which started a fight.

Unlike human fisticuffs, the ghosts had to settle for flinging luminescent ectoplasm at each other, leaving the walls sticky and glowing in their wake. But each day, the report to their boss in the attic was the same; no humans.

Boo took to floating in the garden, up to the brick perimeter, stretching as far as she could go against the enchantment that held them all captive. The others had lost interest in the humans after they hadn't reappeared and had settled back into their old lives of idleness. But Boo couldn't keep still.

She'd had a taste of what it might be like to have company and she couldn't give up on that. She strained her senses to capture snippets of conversations from people passing by the crumbling mansion.

She wondered if the boss would be happy if he knew that the locals were scared of the house; that they turned up their collars as they passed by, even on sunny days. Or that they whispered that a friend of a friend had heard banging and seen lights flashing in the windows at night.

Creak and Giggle would enjoy that. They both seemed to get a sort of sick pleasure from tricking others. Maybe if she told them, they would spend more time thinking up ways to prank humans instead of picking on her.

She moved in parallel to the wall, listening to a small child kick a ball against the bricks when she heard the screech of the old iron gate. It took her a minute to place it and she gazed across the overgrown garden. The left gate had rusted from its hinges and lay propped against the brick wall that marked the boundary of the property. But a man pushed the other open, his legs straining against his corduroy slacks as he pitted himself against the ancient metal. He pushed his untidy hair out of his eyes and shook his head as he took in the property. With a sigh, he turned and headed back to the pavement.

Boo hurried over. She rested on the paved path and peered out through the gate posts. A van was parked right in front of the house. *Richardson's Surveyancing Services*. The surveyor! She did a small somersault in the air before standing right by the gates, watching the van like a hawk sensitive to every movement.

The man reappeared after a couple of minutes. He was now covered in a set of blue overalls. A pair of gloves dangled precariously from one pocket. He took out a rectangular block and started poking at it as he walked up the path. Boo moved closer. Her eyes widened. The man was writing on the rectangle, which gave off a faint glow. She hadn't seen anything like it.

She peeked over his shoulder and caught the words *decrepit* and *overgrown* as he typed.

He walked a complete circuit around the Victorian manor before trying the front door. The ancient hinges squeaked in protest at being pushed open, but the heavy wooden door gave way. Boo followed Richardson inside. He shook his head almost continuously as he wandered from room to room. Occasionally he would bend and tap an area of wall or press in another machine before tapping away on his electronic writing machine. He shook the banister vigorously before he climbed upstairs and let out something like a grunt of satisfaction. Boo watched, fascinated, as he peeled away sections of wallpaper and opened and closed the sash windows. Then he headed for the attic.

Boo froze. Of course, he would go up there. He'd seen the rest of the house. She agonised over what to do. If he went up there, the others would notice him. But maybe that was for the best. Even as she struggled internally, her ethereal body moved to the attic door. The key was in the lock. Using all of her strength, she tried to turn it. She strained, using every ounce of will to get it to move.

Richardson's footsteps sounded on the staircase. She tried again. Come on! Click. The key turned. The attic was locked. She sagged in relief. But that was only half the job. She forced herself back to the door and grunted as she tried to pull the key from the lock. She had to hide it. It slid slowly away from the door and fell to the floor with a metallic clang.

Richardson panted as he reached the top step. The air was stiflingly still inside the house and he'd be glad to be gone. One last room to go. He looked around for the source of the clank he'd heard, sure it had come from up here.

"Hello? Is anyone there?" he shook his head, "Course there isn't." Still muttering to himself, he reached for the brass handle and turned it. It twisted, but the door stayed shut. He tried again, turning the handle back and forth. He swore. Well, he'd looked everywhere else, what could be lurking in the attic. He took a step towards the staircase. The toe of his brown work boot hit something and sent it spinning across the dusty carpet to hit the yellowed skirting board.

"What was that?" Richardson pushed his hand through his brown spiky hair and considered walking away. He swore again. Curiosity got the better of him. He often thought that was one of the reasons he'd become a surveyor, to find out the secrets lurking beneath a property's exterior polish. Of course, in some cases, Richardson thought as he took in the curling wallpaper, the owner didn't bother trying to hide the decay. He shuffled forward, using his phone as a torch to find the mysterious object, now lathered in a layer of dust. It didn't take him long, and he brushed a stray spiderweb out of the way to retrieve the key. He wiped his hands on his overalls, freeing them of the sticky strands of webbing and turned back to the door. He tried the key in the lock. It stuck. Not one to be deterred by a difficult key, Richardson tried again, using his fingers to force the key round. With a loud click, the door unlocked.

He didn't see Boo fly through the door ahead of him. The ghosts buzzed invisibly around Richardson as he walked towards the large round window at the front of the house. He used his sleeve to wipe a circle in the layer of dirt that covered the glass and peered through.

He let out a low whistle as he took in the view of the grounds.

"This place must have been something back in the day."

"My boy, you have no idea." Spookie appeared next to the human and took his turn at the window as Richardson moved away. The human didn't reply. He couldn't see the large, round ghost hovering inches away.

Richardson shone his phone torch around the room, taking in the few cardboard boxes in the attic, the antique chaise longue covered with baroque fabric and threadbare tassels, the old doll's house covered with spider webs, the mirror leaning against a wall, spotted with age. The beam of light seemed to refract oddly as he moved it around the attic, but he didn't think anything of it. He certainly never considered that it might be caused by a quintet of ghosts gathered close by. He looked up at the ceiling before scribbling a note on his tablet; *interior roof seems to be in good condition*.

As he turned to leave, the light glinted off something in the corner of the attic. Richardson frowned and walked over, weaving his way between old boxes stacked precariously on top of each other. He moved one aside, balancing his phone under his chin as he did so, the light waving wildly as he struggled to clamp the phone tightly. The phone dropped to the floor. The light faded to a small patch on the floorboards.

Richardson bent to pick it up. Out of the corner of his eye, he thought he spotted movement. He turned. Nothing. He fumbled with his phone, then shone it across the attic. Something scurried away in the dark. Mice. Something else to put in his survey. Richardson turned back to the small space he had cleared in front of him. He angled his phone and took in the large black trunk he had found. Well made, he thought, with metal casings on the corners and a stout clasp at the front, which he supposed had been what had caught the light.

He squinted as he tried to make out the lettering stamped onto the leather. He wiped away the decades of dust and read aloud, "E. Spook. Huh. Strange name." He took a picture, then hesitated.

Dammit, he was curious and how often did he get to find an old trunk in an attic? He pressed the button on the clasp. It unbuckled instantly and the lid cracked open a tantalising sliver. Richardson reached out and opened it.

# Chapter 3

## In which Spookie suffers a disappointment

The trunk was full of old clothes. The ghosts gathered excitedly as Richardson sifted through the garments.

"My favourite dress!" Boo exclaimed as the man pulled out an evening dress hung with silver beads. She danced across the floor in glee, reminding Spookie of the parties he'd used to host here.

"Hey boss, isn't that your hat?" Tinker pointed to a brown fedora that Richardson had taken out of the trunk. It was in good condition. Richardson studied it and brushed off a piece of lint. He twisted it back and forth in the dim light before lifting it up and studying it more closely. The ghosts drifted closer. Spookie pushed to the front.

He watched as Richardson turned, frowning slightly. The human caught his reflection staring back at him from the dusty mirror and gave himself a lopsided grin. He spun the hat in his hands then stopped. He met his own gaze in the mirror and with a lopsided smile, balanced the fedora in one hand, and lifted it to his brow like a gangster in an old movie.

Spookie couldn't speak. A deathly hush fell in the late afternoon attic. He almost buzzed with anticipation. Try it on, he willed the human, put it on and I can be free of this wretched place. Richardson's hand edged closer to his forehead. Closer. Closer. Less than a centimetre to go.

Spookie's mouth widened into a large grin. He rubbed his hands together, imagining what he'd do when he left the house. He'd fly as fast as his undead form could take him to the park. The warm sun would be warm on his spirit body as he moved along the banks of the river or maybe he'd move amongst the shady trees, pausing to take in the flowers. He could almost smell the sweet scent of the briar roses trailing through the leafy hedgerows.

An electronically synthesised version of Fur Elise broke the tension in the attic. Richardson put the hat back on the chest with one hand while he pulled his phone out of his back pocket and gathered up his tablet.

"Alright boss?...Yeah, yeah, I'm just finishing up…Look, are you sure about this place? …Yeah…No, it all seems sound enough. No damp, no rot, just the usual decorative damage you get in these old houses. It's sturdy as a brick though…No, no problems, it's just, I dunno, there's something about this place, gives me the creeps."

The ghosts could hear the tinny laughter through the small speaker on the phone, followed by a muffled voice.

"Yeah, maybe you're right. I have been watching a few horror films lately. Alright, I'm on my way out. I'll send you the report this evening. Ta-ra." With a shake of his head, Richardson made his way out of the attic, leaving the door open behind him.

"No!" shrieked Spookie. His anger was palpable. The air in the attic swirled furiously, responding to his energy. The door slammed shut, rattling the door frame dangerously. From the stairwell, Richardson swore, and they heard him descending more quickly.

The whirlwind of energy dissipated as quickly as it began. Spookie sank to the floor, exhausted by his exertions. The others crowded round nervously. It was rare for the large ghost to lose his temper and they hadn't seen the full force of his anger since he'd discovered he'd been trapped in the attic. It was the witch's last joke; to make sure that the man who loved the outdoors was cooped up inside for eternity.

"It'll be OK boss, you'll see." Tinker edged closer and laid a reassuring hand on the ghost's back.

"OK? OK?!" Spookie exploded. "Explain to me exactly how it will be OK?! We're all trapped here as long as that hat stays in this ghoulforsaken attic! And that idiot was our one chance to be free of this place! The only person to venture into this room in seventy years and now he's gone. So how exactly do you think that it'll be OK?" Tinker winced at the sarcasm laced onto the last word. He moved away to the window and watched Richardson scurry down the garden path to his van.

Tinker turned back to his boss, who had deflated back to the floor. The smaller ghost's blueish tinge glowed more brightly as the idea took hold.

"This could be a good thing…"

Spookie looked up from his spot on the floor about to shout at his friend, but a spark in Tinker's eyes stopped him. Instead, he gestured for Tinker to go on.

"Think about it, boss. If someone buys this place, they'll want to do it up, right? And what does that mean?"

"What does it mean?" Creak interrupted sharply, not seeing where Tinker was going.

"It means more people will come to the house." Tinker looked around triumphantly.

"So?"

"So, more people means more chances that someone will pick up the hat and take it out of the attic, which means…"

"I'll be free. We'll all be free!" Spookie could feel the small seed of hope start to grow inside him. He was cautious. He hadn't nurtured the seed in so many long years, he had thought it was long dead, shrivelled up like the uncared-for houseplant in the library and instead it had lain dormant, waiting for the right conditions so it could bloom again. A small smile played around his ghostly lips. "Then we'd better get ready for some guests."

# Chapter 4

## In which realisation dawns

A further week passed. The ghosts had put their excited energy into thinking up ways to encourage people up the stairs. Boo had practiced moving objects until she could carry the red and white china vase halfway upstairs before she had to put it down, exhausted by the weight of the corporeal object.

Creak had taken to hiding himself away in the green bedroom, preferring to be alone. None of the others had any idea what he was doing but strange noises emanated from behind the dark wooden door at all times of the day and night. Giggle had ventured in once and had left the room shaking. He refused to speak about what he might have seen, and merely shook his head and smiled his inane grin when questioned.

Tinker concocted scheme after scheme in his mind, sometimes sharing his ideas with the others. Soon, the other ghosts started avoiding him. Only Boo indulged his bright mind, listening to the plans and nodding along as she practiced moving the toys left in the dolls' house.

And all the time Spookie floated back and forth in the middle of the attic, waiting. If he had had feet, he would have worn a path on the dull floorboards. Instead, there was barely a wisp of dust as he moved about the room. Despite common sense telling him to keep his hope tightly in check, it had unfurled and blossomed until every day the house stayed empty seemed like a new torture.

It reminded him of when he'd first realised his fate. He hadn't taken it seriously when the witch had cursed him and his 'stupid hat'. Whoever heard of a curse having power? But it had. Whatever black magic she had used had bound him to the fedora he had worn in life. A ghostly remnant of it still topped his spirit form but that didn't matter. It was the real thing that was his torment.

That curse meant he had to stay within a few feet of the damn object. That gave him the run of the attic, but he couldn't leave. Ever. He'd spent years trying to outfox the curse. He was sure that there was a loophole, if he could only find it the way he'd found loopholes in contracts, the way he'd wheedled deals to his advantage. His team had helped him as best they could, humouring every one of his schemes. Tinker had come up with new ideas daily and the ghosts had tried to execute them. To no avail. Nothing changed.

He paused in his pacing to glare at the hat. He'd been so proud of it when he was alive, so cocksure when he wore it. It was part of his armour. It told people not to mess with him, that he was a man of business. Now he was torn between loathing it and longing for it to be his freedom. With a snort of frustration, he resumed his path just as Boo and Giggle came careening in.

"Someone's here!"

Spookie turned and stared at them. "You sure?"

The ghosts nodded eagerly, their heads bobbing in tandem. Spookie flew to the window and stared out of the dust covered glass. Workmen in brown overalls strode along the garden path carrying toolboxes and heavy-duty equipment. Spookie recognised several of the tools; his business had sometimes required the judicious application of a crowbar to make sure that things ran smoothly.

"Well, what are yoos all doing here? Go on, find out what they are doing."

"Yes, boss."

Spookie watched the ghosts as they scurried out of the room to follow the workmen. He turned back to the window, watching helplessly. What he wouldn't give to leave the attic, to go downstairs and roam the house freely with the rest of ghosts? And maybe, just maybe, if one of the workmen – or workwomen, he noticed, with a shake of his head – found his hat, he'd be able to leave this dusty room.

Click. And the door opened, and someone walked through. No, two someone's. Spookie drifted closer.

"What do they want us to do in here?"

"Nothing." The older man shook his head as he consulted a list clipped onto a clipboard. "Looks like this is going to be storage."

The younger man rubbed the back of his head. "Well then, I guess we'd better tidy up so we can store stuff here."

The workmen began by selecting a box and moving it from one side of the room to another. One of them picked up the doll and stared at it.

"This thing gives me the creeps."

"Just don't look it in the eye, or it might possess you."

They both laughed at that. Spookie smiled at the irony of it. If all went well, he would possess one of them soon enough.

The younger worker, the one with the dirty blonde hair, tossed the doll behind a storage box and they continued to stack boxes until the floor in the middle was completely clear.

"Hey what's this?"

The older worker reached for the hat, newly revealed. Spookie hung next to him, waiting. If he could breathe, he would have held his breath. With a brush of his hand, the worker shoved it behind a trunk and the pair moved the last of the boxes into a neat tower before heading back downstairs to help with the rest of the renovations.

Spookie stared at the tower of boxes. He flew through them. His hat sat on the floor, dented and covered with dust. He floated back and forth through the boxes.

More workers tramped upstairs. They deposited gilt-framed pictures and chipped antiques in the newly cleared space.

Unseen, Spookie hovered, willing them to look behind the trunk. But the humans kept stacking boxes, piling up pictures until there was no floor visible in the abandoned attic. Spookie let out a scream of frustration. There was no way that anyone would find the hat now. He was doomed to live his life here in the attic.

Wave after wave of fury coursed through his translucent body, calling the others to him.

"You alright boss?"

Spooky turned to face his minions. They all drifted back away from him in terror.

"If they won't let me leave here, then I won't let them stay."

# Chapter 5

## The Grand Opening

Despite the ghosts' best effort, the workers had finished the renovations. True, the disappearing tools had baffled them and strange noises that bubbled through the house whenever anyone had a late shift were creepy. The humans soon avoided working in the old house after nightfall, and no amount of floodlights or overtime bonuses could persuade them to stay.

It was bad enough during the daytime. Nothing quite explained the strange prickling sensation on the backs of the workers' necks, as if they were being watched by an invisible presence. But there was never anybody there. The builders and decorators had all been glad to leave and put the strange, old house behind them with a wry shake of the head and a good story to tell down the pub.

And now it was the day of the grand opening. It had been feted for weeks as the destination hotel in the city. The owner had deigned to do interviews with local and national press, always interested in what a billionaire did with his money. When asked, the owner had simply smiled and said the house reminded him of somewhere he'd visited as a child.

Guests milled around in the grand reception hall, made of the original entrance hall and the pale-yellow drawing room knocked through. Glasses of champagne in hands, they smiled and congratulated the owner on the successful completion of his project as the setting sun reflected through the stained glass in the front door to create colourful patterns on the hardwood floors.

Then a smiling attendant took the invitees on a tour of the building. The guests 'oohed' and 'aahed' over the décor; tasteful yet opulent with wallpaper patterns, refurbished fireplaces and fancy chandeliers harking back to the building's Victorian heyday.

The interior designer, Lars, had scoured the attic for 'finishing touches' and had rehung many of the original paintings. No one on the design team commented that the pictures weren't in the same rooms they had placed them in. Instead, guests smiled and congratulated Lars on the masterful placement of the pieces and he smiled back, blinking furiously as he downed his champagne.

Back in reception, after the tour, the attendant smiled. "And now, ladies and gentlemen, it's time for our first guests to check in and settle down for the night."

Those not lucky enough to have got a room left the party and promised themselves that they would book as soon as they could. The others, mostly members of the press, and a family who had won a competition in the national papers, checked in and carried their bags upstairs to get ready for the night as dusk fell.

# Chapter 6

## In which the ghosts attempt to scare the guests

Upstairs in the attic, the setting sun meant that the ghosts were getting ready too.

"OK yoos lot, I know yoos all been practicing, and I know you can do it. You're going to scare 'em out but good. This is our house and it's going to stay our house!"

The ghosts whooped. Giggle did a loop the loop and zoomed through the floor. Creak and Tinker followed, but Boo stayed.

"You sure about this, boss?"

Spookie floated over to her. "Boo, you're the best of us, you know that, but after how they disrespected us, destroying our home, making sure we could never leave, well it's too much. If we was alive, you know what we'd do."

Boo nodded. She knew. And it wasn't always pretty.

"Well, we ain't got that option anymore, so we gotta do what we can and show these humans that this is our turf. Got it?"

"Yes, boss." Boo drifted through the floor to her rooms.

The ghosts had decided to divvy up the guestrooms so they could get as many people out as possible in one night. Her first room was the first floor, on the right.

She hesitated outside, then floated through the locked wooden door. Inside, a single man clicked a remote as scenes changed on a slim black box. Boo paused next to his bed and watched the moving pictures, entranced by the colourful people dancing in the shiny picture frame, it was some sort of magic for sure, like the tablet the surveyor had used.

The man reached out for a glass of water on the bedside table. His hand passed through Boo's insubstantial form.

"Argh!" she exclaimed.

"Ugh," the man said, staring at his hand. "What the heck?" He moved his hand back and forth through the spot where Boo stood. "It's so cold!"

Boo moved back, her face a picture of disgust as she gagged. If she had a stomach, she was sure the contents would spew from her mouth.

"Weird…" The man grabbed a small rectangle and began tapping away at it. Boo drifted closer. It was similar to the device the surveyor had used, only smaller…and there were numbers on it. Was it a phone?

Tinker flew through the wall. "How ya doing, Boo? Need a hand? Me and Giggle teamed up on this one couple. Ha! I think they've checked out already!"

"No, I got this."

"OK Boo-bear, catch ya later." Tinker floated upwards until he disappeared through the ceiling, causing the chandelier to rattle.

"What?" The man looked up at the rocking light fitting.

Boo shook her head. Time to get scaring. She moved back to the bedside table and looked at the man, then she turned to his drink. She concentrated and pushed her hand through the glass. The water cooled and cracked until it was ice. She smiled with satisfaction.

He heard the tinkle and stared at the frozen glass. He picked it up. "Fascinating…"

"No, it's not fascinating. It's scary!" Boo huffed.

The small ghost floated over to the pictures on the wall. She focused, groaning at the effort as she rattled the paintings one by one. She got a bit carried away on the last one and it fell to the floor with a thud.

The man crab walked backwards along the bed until his back pressed against the upholstered headboard.

Boo smiled; that was more like it.

"Wh-who's there?" The guest waved the remote control like a weapon.

Boo flew through the TV. She shuddered at the electric current. The picture flickered to static and back again.

"Is someone here?"

Boo felt her energy drain. She couldn't keep this up much longer. Gathering herself, she tried her new trick and spoke. Her voice echoed around the room. "Get out! Get out!"

The man screamed and raced out of his bedroom.

Boo sighed. The first time she'd communicated with a living being and she'd scared them away. Surely there was a better way, she thought as she drifted back to the attic to share her success with the others.

Spookie's laugh rolled around the attic like thunder as the ghosts relayed their scares. Tinker and Giggle re-enacted their scare of a couple who had locked themselves in the bathroom and sobbed before racing out of the hotel.

"And you, Creak?"

Creak's smile widened. "Oh, I scared him good, boss. He'll be gone by morning."

# Chapter 7

*In which the ghosts realise it's not as simple as it seemed*

**M**orning came and the four ghosts left Spookie to his attic prison. Boo trailed behind the others as they zoomed downstairs to the reception desk. The young lady's hair bobbed as she bent her head over the desk and drew thick lines through the names of guests in the ledger in front of her. She took a deep breath and plastered on a smile as a man entered, wearing a crisp shirt.

Boo thought he looked familiar.

"Good morning, sir."

"How did it go?" He rubbed his hands together.

The woman tucked a piece of hair behind her ear. "Three of them checked out. Only the Morrisons and the man in room four are left…"

"What do you mean, they checked out?"

The woman swallowed and Boo shrank back at the force of the man's anger.

"They said they hadn't paid to stay in a haunted hotel…"

"Haunted! People stay in an old house, there are bound to be a few bumps and strange noises in the night. It's just the building settling."

"They said they had chills and–"

"What? Are they in a musical? It's an old house, bound to be a few draughts. I stayed here, didn't I? I suppose you refunded them too?"

"Yes, sir. Sorry, sir. Do you want me to call the press team?"

There was a long pause. "No, I'll call them. And I'll stay again tonight, after all, it wouldn't look good if the owner checked out after guests have fled."

"The boss isn't going to like this," Tinker said.

Giggle shook his head and floated to the window. "We should get back upstairs and prepare for tonight."

The two of them floated through the ceiling. Boo headed upwards, but stopped as she reached the chandelier.

"Creak?"

The ghost was staring at the man, his face a picture of fury. Boo followed his gaze. The man – the owner – crossed the hall, went into the breakfast room, and helped himself to a piece of toast from the buffet table.

Creak turned to her, and Boo shrank back, putting the sparkling glass light fixture between her and the spirit. "He didn't leave."

"What do you mean?"

"The man I scared. That's him."

"Maybe…"

"I've got to go." With that, Creak dashed out of the room.

Boo shook her head and drifted back to the attic.

"…How? You told me yoos did your best, right?" His eyes narrowed. "You did do your best?"

Giggle and Tinker nodded.

"Then I don't understand why they stayed."

"Maybe they calmed down."

Spookie turned to Boo. "What?"

"After we scared them, maybe they calmed down. I mean, when I left, I didn't have any energy left, so maybe we can't scare everyone out."

"You're right, little Boo. Maybe I expected too much of yoos all. Rest now, and tonight I'll use my energy to give you all a favour." Spookie beamed around the attic, then frowned. "Where's Creak?"

They all shrugged as best they could. "Well, someone find him and tell him to get here just after sunset. I want yoos all ready to get rid of those humans."

# Chapter 8

## In which there is a big scare

That evening, the ghosts lined up in front of Spookie. He lifted his shapeless hands over each of them in turn. Boo shivered as he reached her. His power trickled through her like ice water, chilling her spirit.

"Go out and know that yoos all have my favour!"

Tinker, Creak, and Giggle raced to the door. Boo followed.

"Boo, a moment."

Tinker shot her a pitying gaze before he disappeared through the wood.

Boo turned. "Yes, boss."

He floated over to her. "I'm worried about Creak. He's acting strange. Can you check up on him tonight, kid? Stay with him?"

"Of course, but…"

Spookie raised a spectral eyebrow.

"But I won't be able to scare anyone else out if I'm with him."

"Nonsense. Scare out someone first, then go help him and keep an eye on him. Make sure he knows what he has to do."

Boo nodded.

She floated down to her first room. Two young girls slept soundly in matching twin beds. They looked so sweet; hair plaited in pigtails to keep it neat while they were asleep. She approached the bed, as silent as the grave. If she'd lived, maybe she'd have had children. Two little angels like these. They even had her mousy brown hair colour.

Unable to help herself, she reached out and brushed the cheek of the one nearest to her. The girl shivered and pulled her duvet tighter. She opened her eyes.

"Leave me alone, Bella." The older child threw a pillow at her younger sister.

"AAAH!" Bella screamed. She switched on the light and glared over at her sister. "Why did you do that?"

Boo sighed. The girls were awake now. Might as well get it over with. At least it was her and not one of the others. She shuddered to think what Giggle might dream up for these sleeping beauties.

She noticed the doll cuddled up next to the child; that wouldn't be too scary. She concentrated and lifted it, so it sat upright. Bella's eyes widened and she pointed.

Her sister turned and then sat very still. "M…Molly? Are you moving?"

Boo forced the doll's head forward to make it nod. But she applied too much pressure, and the head came away from the neck. It rolled forward into the child's lap.

The girl screamed and leaped from the bed. Both girls huddled together against the wall, chests heaving.

It wasn't meant to go like this. Boo picked up the head and floated over to the bed to try to reattach it to the body. The girls screamed again.

Giggle stuck his head through the wall. "What's going on in here?"

Boo wailed in frustration. Nothing was going right. "Leave me alone!" She shouted and forced out all her power to push the other ghost away. Giggle shot backwards, his mouth a surprised 'o' as her power expanded and formed a ghostly barrier around the room.

Boo backed away. "I'm sorry," she whispered to the terrified girls. Then she fled.

She stopped outside the door and slumped onto the carpet, trembling and ashamed of herself and what she had done. This couldn't be right. Somewhere downstairs, a clock struck one. She sniffed. Maybe she could get to Creak and stop him, at least.

Boo knew exactly where the ghost would be. He was as puffed up as a peacock when he'd been alive and not being able to scare out the owner would have pricked his pride. She hurried along the corridor to the largest suite and ducked into the room.

She pulled up as soon as she crossed the threshold. The owner cowered on his bed as Creak towered over him, a vision of shadow and fangs. The human's breath puffed out in small clouds in the icy room.

"No," Boo's voice was barely audible.

As if the man could hear her, he turned and stared straight at her, his eyes wide and white, his skin clammy with fear. He could see her, she knew it, the same as when he'd looked at her in the lobby months ago. This could all go differently. If people could see them, then they could explain. They could help Spookie and all of them to leave. But they wouldn't help if the ghosts scared them out.

"No! Creak!" She reached to pull the ghost back, but it was too late. He puffed up further. The ghost's eyes glowed blood red and he dived at the man, conjuring snakes and spiders before him. The human shrieked and threw up his hands to protect his head. Creak laughed and span round the room, knocking Boo aside. She felt so weak as she span through the air. With her fading energy, she gripped the door and flung it open.

"Run!"

"Yes," shouted Creak. "Run!" He hounded after the owner, sending shadows writhing at the man's feet as he fled.

# Chapter 9

*In which the ghosts realise they've gone too far*

Spookie laughed long and loud as Creak regaled them yet again with the story of how he had spent the night scaring the owner until he had run, screaming like a banshee, out of the house. Only Boo kept her mouth tightly shut, ashamed of what they had become.

They hadn't been saints when they were alive, of course, but they had a sort of code and terrorising innocent people wasn't part of it. They had settled disputes and protected their territory, sure, but they had never stooped so low. Spookie's team had never needed to do much more than raise an eyebrow to make a point, and Spookie had always been open to compromise.

"Not enjoying the story, Boo-bear?" teased Creak. "You helped."

"I don't think it's right. I think we could live together." She crossed her arms over her chest.

Spookie moved to her side and wrapped an arm around her. "Hey kid, you know this wasn't what I wanted. But what choice do we have? They have trapped us here; we had no say in that. And they have changed our home, again without consulting us. It's rude. It's disrespectful and I won't tolerate disrespect."

"But these people don't even know–"

"Hush, Boo. I've made up my mind. I want all of yoos to be as scary as Creak here. Now, tell it again."

Boo turned her back on the group and went to the window. She blinked twice as the van pulled up. "Er, guys."

They ignored her, and she repeated herself.

"What is it, Boo, scared of your own shadow now?"

She narrowed her eyes at Giggle. "We got company."

Spookie pushed her aside and squinted out of the window. A van had pulled up outside the gates and four tall figures in beige work suits marched down the path carrying black boxes. "Go see what it is!" Spookie waved them away.

Boo sped downstairs and peered out the window, pressing her face up to the glass. The large lettering on the side of the van read 'Ghost Research Unit – ghosts getting you down? Give GRU a call for all your spiritual needs'.

# Chapter 10

### In which one of the ghosts is captured

I t's not a problem, boss." Creak soothed Spookie, "We'll scare them out, just like the others."

"Yeah, yeah, we can do it."

"Of course yoos can! And these busters must be the last resort. So, we get rid of them and that's it. Peace and quiet."

"They're only here because we scared people," Boo sulked.

"Boo, we all gotta be in on this. These people are professionals. I need to know you're on my team. You're with me, ain't you Boo?"

Boo looked into Spookie's eyes. The same eyes that had seen something in her and taken her in when he could have thrown her on the street. She'd pledged to do anything in her power to protect him then, not knowing that it would cost her life and, worse than that, her death. "Of course."

"Good girl. So, here's the plan…"

Boo's attention wandered. Of course, she wanted to protect Spookie, but he didn't realise the dark path he was on. He couldn't leave the attic, so he hadn't seen the monster that Creak had become, that all of them were becoming. Boo wanted to save him, save all of them, so she had her own plan. Because, if these people were professionals, then she could contact them.

She spent the day hovering around the ghost hunters. Their equipment beeped when she flew through it, but all they did was note down readings and murmur "Fascinating." One of them, a woman, wandered about the house asking for 'contact with the spirits'.

"We want to help, knock twice if you can hear me."

She couldn't stop the grin that spread over her face. They were here to help, she knew it. But her powers weren't strong enough to 'knock twice' to show she was here. Didn't they know that ghosts were more powerful at night?

More than once, the other ghosts had caught her close to the instruments and Tinker, for sure, wasn't buying her ditzy girl act.

"What are you playing at, Boo?"

"Nothing, I'm curious is all. They're such interesting machines."

He gave her a look. One that said he didn't believe her. "You were never interested in the machines I created when we were alive."

She rested a hand on his translucent arm. "I was interested in everything you did. But don't you wonder if things could be different? If we could make peace, maybe even free Spookie?"

Tinker shook his head. "We're past that now, Boo. We gotta do this. It's the only way we can be free to live here as we want."

Boo moved away from him. He cupped her face with his hands. "Just make sure you're in the game tonight, OK?"

"Of course I will be. Where else would I be?"

That night, as she promised, Boo was there with the other ghosts, all hyped up on Spookie's power that he had leant them.

"Alright then, follow my lead." Creak went in first. The others followed. A moment of quiet anticipation flooded Boo as they surrounded the first ghostbuster. His beige overalls swished as he moved around the room. His hand patted a small box with a door in the top that dangled from his belt. Before the others had a chance to act, Boo moved forward. This was her chance. The chance to save them all. She used her energy to appear in the closest thing she could to a corporeal form.

"Hi, pleased to meet you." She smiled and held out her hand.

The ghost hunter screamed and ran out of the room.

"Whatchoo playing at, Boo? We had a plan."

She looked down at the floor. "I thought–"

"Stop thinking and follow the plan! Now we've gotta find another one." Creak pushed past her and walked through the wall into another room.

Tinker shook his head. Boo looked away. She couldn't cope with his disappointment. The small ghost snuffled then followed the others. She would have to be more careful, but maybe she could still make contact.

In the next room, a woman lay on the bed with her eyes closed, wearing the same beige overalls. Creak nudged Tinker and the smaller ghost flew over and ran his hand over her face. Goose-pimples appeared on her skin, but she stayed motionless on the bed.

Tinker looked to Creak, who motioned for him to try again. Tinker did and this time the woman's eyes shot open. She flung back the covers and revealed the box hidden there. She punched a large red button on the side and the small doors flew open, sending a cone of light into the room.

Tinker yelled and spiralled around in the beam of light. They had caught him. Creak and Giggle backed away, eyes wide and lips trembling. Not Tinker, thought Boo. He was the best of them. She launched herself forward at the box, pulling her ghostly energy to her palms. She shoved. It fell onto the floor and the beam angled away from her friend.

Tinker shot to a corner of the room, as far as he could get from the box. Boo smiled at him. She moved to go to him, wanting to reassure him that he was free now. But she was stuck. She looked down. The light had her. She opened her mouth to scream as the machine whirled her round and round.

"Yes!" The human punched the air. "We got one! I can't wait to study you. There's so much we don't know about ghosts and I'm the first to catch one!"

Boo stared as she whipped round. Fury coursed through her. She glowed more and more intensely, and then she found that she could stop spinning. She hovered in the light, staring down at the woman celebrating below.

"I wanted to help! I wanted to help everyone!" Boo swelled as she shouted, her anger fuelling her and causing her voice to boom around the room. "But you want to trap us. To study us instead of helping us." She plunged into the machine and the power source flickered out. Boo erupted out of the box and towered over the woman; her face contorted into a vision of vengeance. The ghost raised her arms and darkness spread out in front of her.

The ghost hunter swallowed and stepped back.

"You will leave. Everyone will leave!"

The tendrils of pure dark stretched out from Boo and covered the room with a layer of darkness so deep it seemed more than the mere absence of light, it was the shades of nightmares.

The ghost hunter scrabbled to escape, unable to see. She whimpered and crashed into a table, sending an ornament smashing to the floor.

Boo's voice roared through the house, as her power spread. "Get out! Leave us alone!"

The other ghosts shrunk back from her scare as the hunters fled, screaming into the night.

# Epilogue

## In which there is a new arrival

A knock sounded through the night. Boo raced through the house, Tinker at her side. They reached the front door, and she got into place, a smile playing across her lips.

Spookie had been right. The humans had never wanted to help and so their only option was to get rid of them. Her only regret was the lack of company, but if the alternative was being used like a lab rat, then she knew what she had to do.

She nodded at her friend. Tinker opened the door slowly, allowing it to creak. Boo arranged herself into a giant snake and struck from the shadows. She stopped as if someone had hit her. The shock forced her from her transformation, back into her normal form.

Standing in the doorway wasn't a human, it was a grey figure smelling of decay and mould. One eye hung from its socket, shining in the soft moonlight.

Tinker floated to her side, eyes wide. The new arrival looked from ghost to ghost and smiled, revealing yellowed teeth.

"Hullo there, I hear this is a safe place for supernatural beings? That you don't tolerate humans here." Hope sounded in his soft voice.

Boo and Tinker looked at each other and grinned.

"No, we don't. But you're very welcome. Let me show you around. Perhaps you'd like to see the garden."

# Thank You

A special thank you to Bevan and Gino for their amazing game, which was the inspiration behind this story. And thanks to my amazing patreons: Emma Ward and Mark Canty who always support me.

If you want to support Gemma, please leave a review and you can find her on www.patreon.com/G_Clatworthy for exclusive first reads of new stories.

You can also join her newsletter at www.gemmaclatworthy.com for a free prequel to her Rise of the Dragons series and follow Gemma on www.instagram.com/gemmaclatworthy, www.facebook.com/gemmaclatworthy or join the Facebook reader's group Gemma's book wyrms.

# Other Books by G Clatworthy

Books in the Rise of the Dragons series:

Awakening

Solstice of Dragons

Equinox Betrayal

Darkest Deception

Attack on Avalon

Fated Bloodlines


Books in the Omensford series (set in the Rise of the Dragons universe):

Bedsocks and Broomsticks

Cream Teas and Crystal Balls

Donkeys and Demons

Pumpkins and Popstars

# Children's Books

**The Child Who series:**

The Girl Who Lost Her Listening Ears

The Boy Who Lost His Listening Ears

The Girl Who Dreamed of Sleep

The Boy Who Dreamed of Sleep

**Nanny Pastry series:**

Nanny Pastry and the Nimble Ninjabread Man

**Other books:**

Coronavirus in the words of children

# About the Author

Gemma started writing during the 2020 lockdown and loves fantasy fiction and dragons in particular. She lives in Wiltshire with her family and two cats and also enjoys crafts of all kinds. You can see all her writing on www.patreon.com/G_Clatworthy. Join the conversation at Gemma's book wyrms readers' group on Facebook.

She also writes children's books. You can find out more on her website www.gemmaclatworthy.com or follow her on Instagram (www.instagram.com/gemmaclatworthy) or Facebook (www.facebook.com/gemmaclatworthy).

# TINKERB�T
## GAMES

www.tinkerbotgames.com

Ghostel is a semi-cooperative family game for 2-4 players that plays in 60 minutes.

Prey on the phobias of guests by turning into their worst nightmares. Work with other ghosts to combine forces, and scare away the hardiest of hotel patrons to earn upgrades and get even scarier!

The randomised guest and dice roll mechanic means each round is different from the next, but there's more than luck to winning the game.

Are you the scariest ghost of the night?

Ghostel has been awarded the Dice Tower Seal of Approval!

# TINKERB⚄T
## GAMES

www.tinkerbotgames.com

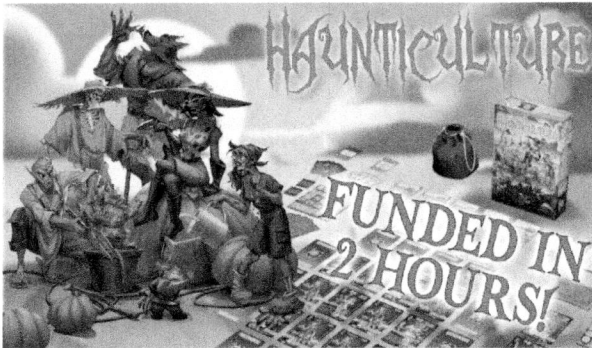

Ghostly gardeners compete to plant the spookiest flowerbed. A 60 min, 1-4 player bidding and tile placement game.

# Tinkerbot Tables

www.tinkerbotgames.com

Handcrafted from solid sustainably sourced wood. High quality that costs less than you think.

Since 2014 we have been hand making tables for customers, working with them to achieve exactly what they want to make their gaming experience truly memorable, but also practical. If you ever played Twilight Imperium or a similar epic game, then you know the pain of pausing mid-way through. That's why this table range was created. We are constantly adding to it and adding more accessories – you have an idea, let us know and we can make it.

Printed in Great Britain
by Amazon

39889247R00047